FAIRY TALE Mini-Unit

These are "repetitive" fairy tales. Each story has a refrain that childen love to hear and to repeat over and over again. The stories are also wonderful for dramatic play.

Read several versions of the following stories to your class:

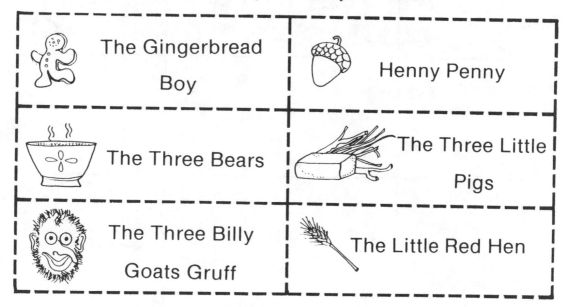

The Gingerbread Boy	Henny Penny
The Three Bears	The Three Little Pigs
The Three Billy Goats Gruff	The Little Red Hen

Directions for Worksheets:

Pages 2-11   Directions are printed at the top of each of these pages.

Pages 12-14   These pages become a mini-picture book of fairy tales for students to take home to share with their parents and siblings.

    1. Each child will need two 9" x 12" sheets of construction paper. Fold the papers in half and staple together to form a book.

    2. Give each child a copy of page 12. Children will cut out and paste the book title to the front page of their book. Paste one story title to the bottom of each page.

    3. Give each child a copy of pages 13 and 14. Color the pictures and paste them to the correct page in the story book.

Pages 15-16   Reproduce these pages on tag or cardstock. The cards can be cut apart and used as a "matching puzzle" by individual children (with three cards forming a set). OR...use the cards along with the gameboard on the back cover as a small group activity with an aide or volunteer helper.

Back cover:

Each player will need a square of colored paper to use as a marker. Player draws a card. If he/she can name the character or object, move one space on the board. If he/she can name the character or object and name the story it comes from, move two spaces. The first player to reach home on the other side of the forest is the winner.

       1

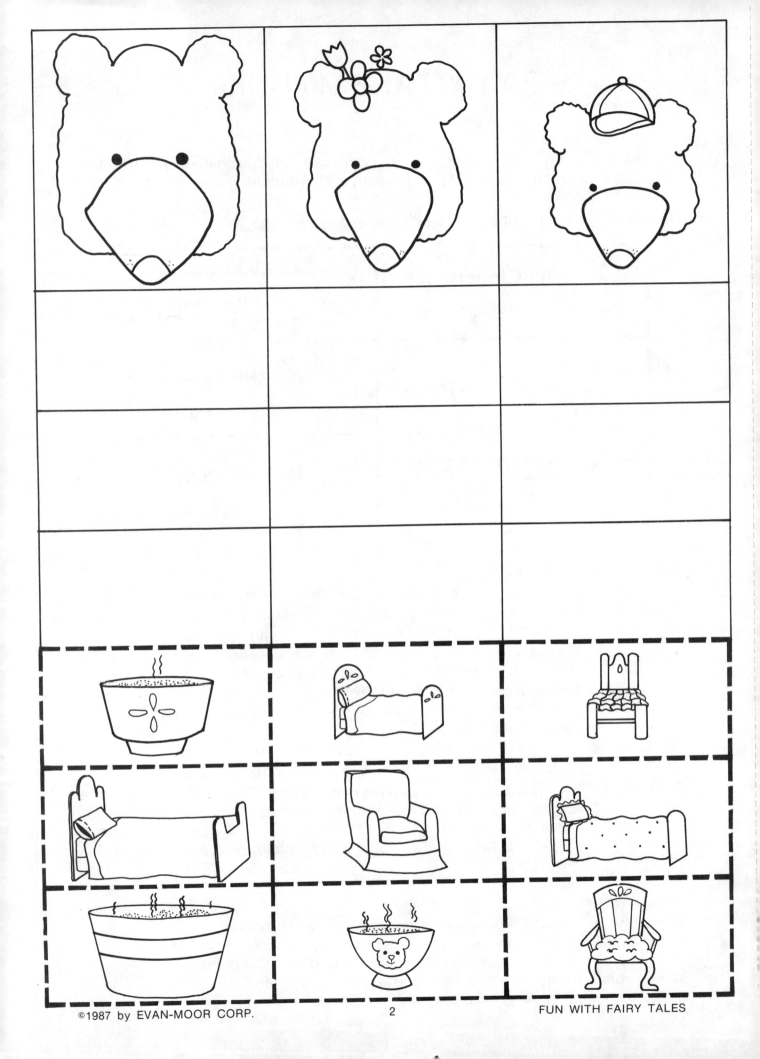

FUN WITH FAIRY TALES

Teacher: Children will trace Goldilock's path through the bears' house.

The Three Bears

3

Teacher: Children color, cut out, and paste the goats and the troll in the picture.

paste

paste

The Three Billy Goats Gruff

paste

paste

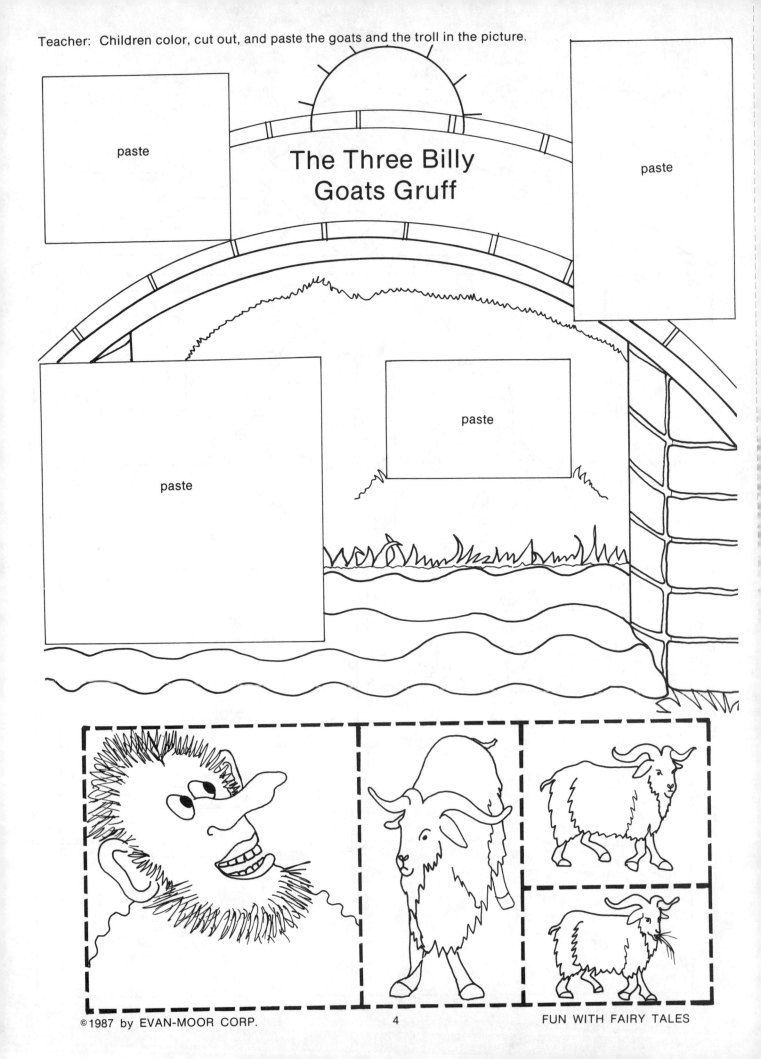

4

Teacher: Children take the Gingerbread Boy through the maze to the edge of the river where he meets the fox. (Why not make your own gingerbread boys to enjoy while hearing this story.)

The Gingerbread Boy

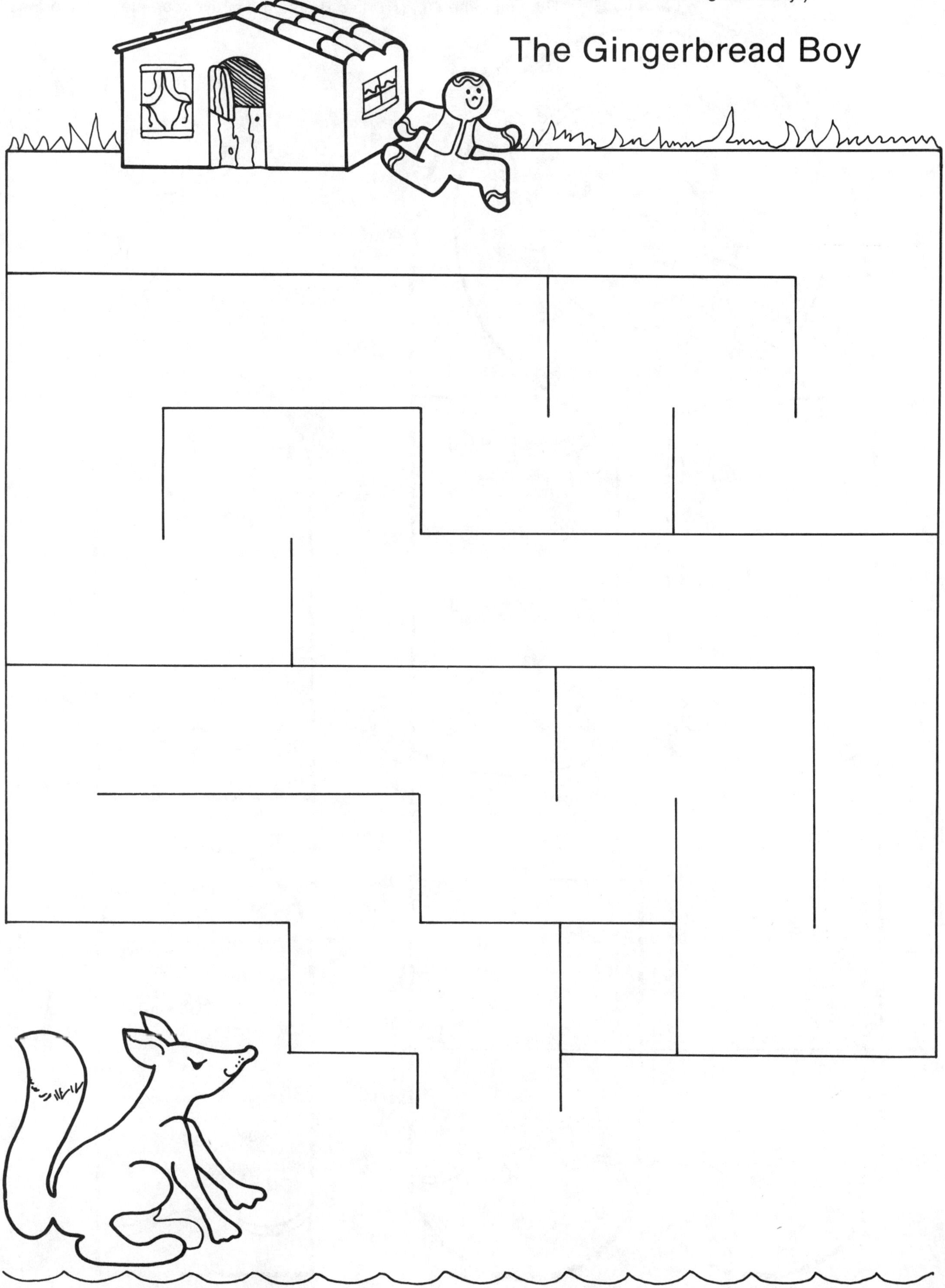

Teacher: Reproduce this page on construction paper. You will need to provide 2 paper fasteners and a drinking straw for each child. The pieces are to be colored, cut out, and connected with the paper fasteners. Then tape the Gingerbread Boy to the straw to create a little puppet.

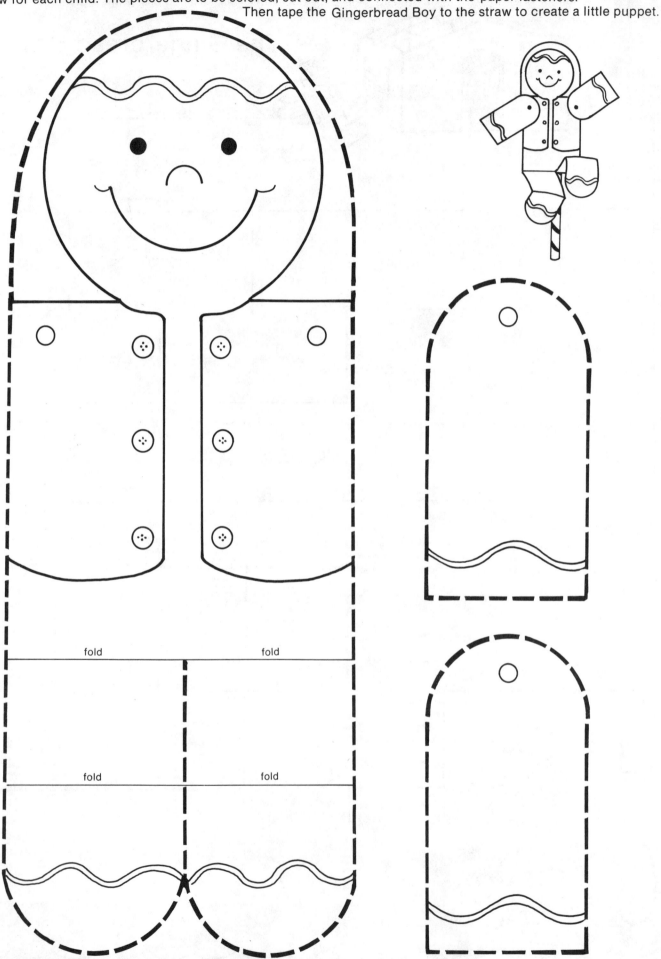

fold   fold

fold   fold

6   FUN WITH FAIRY TALES

The Three Little Pigs

Cut   Fold   Push

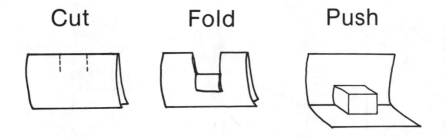

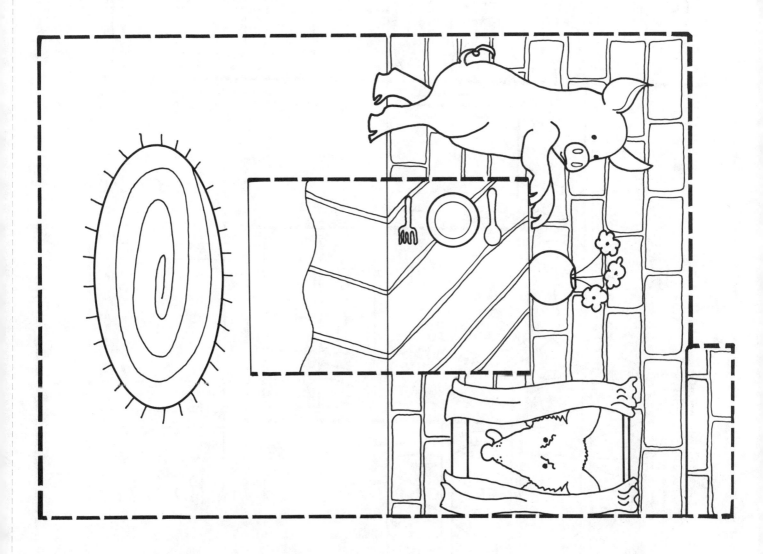

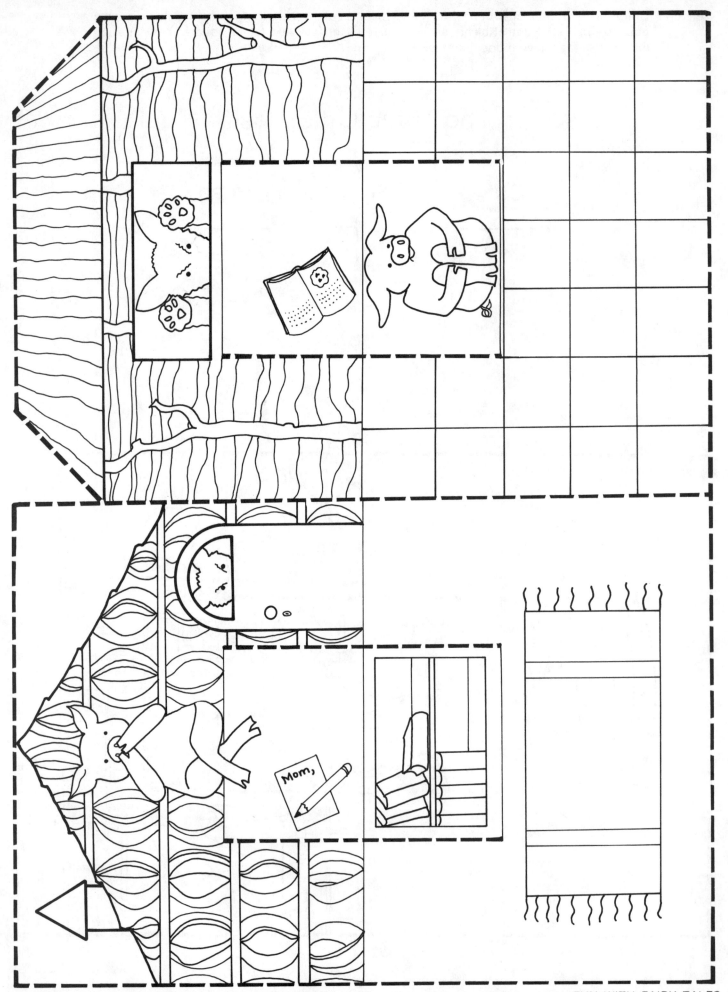

What goes

airy Tales

Fun With I

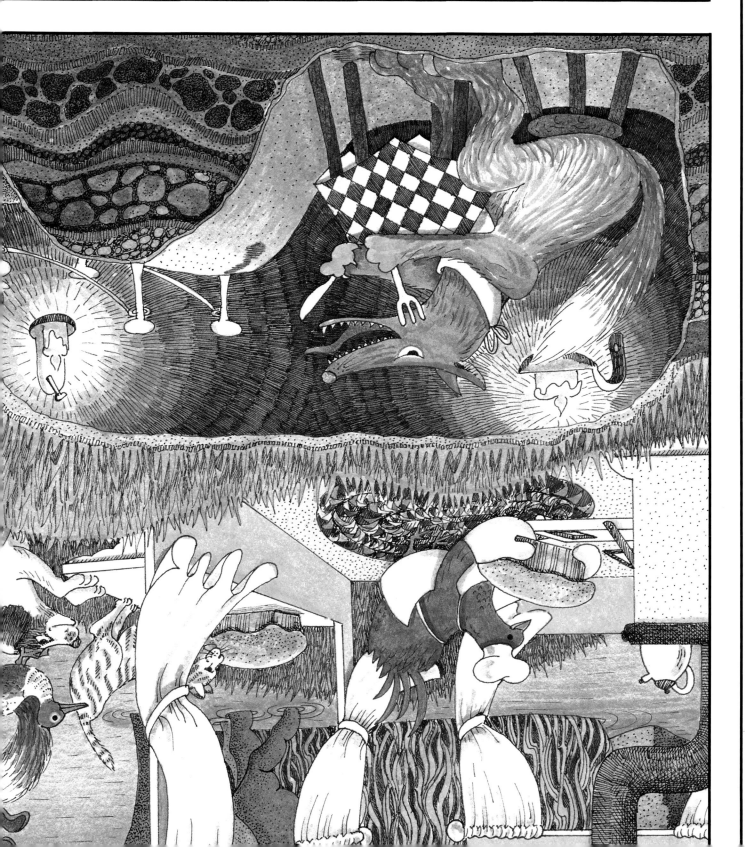

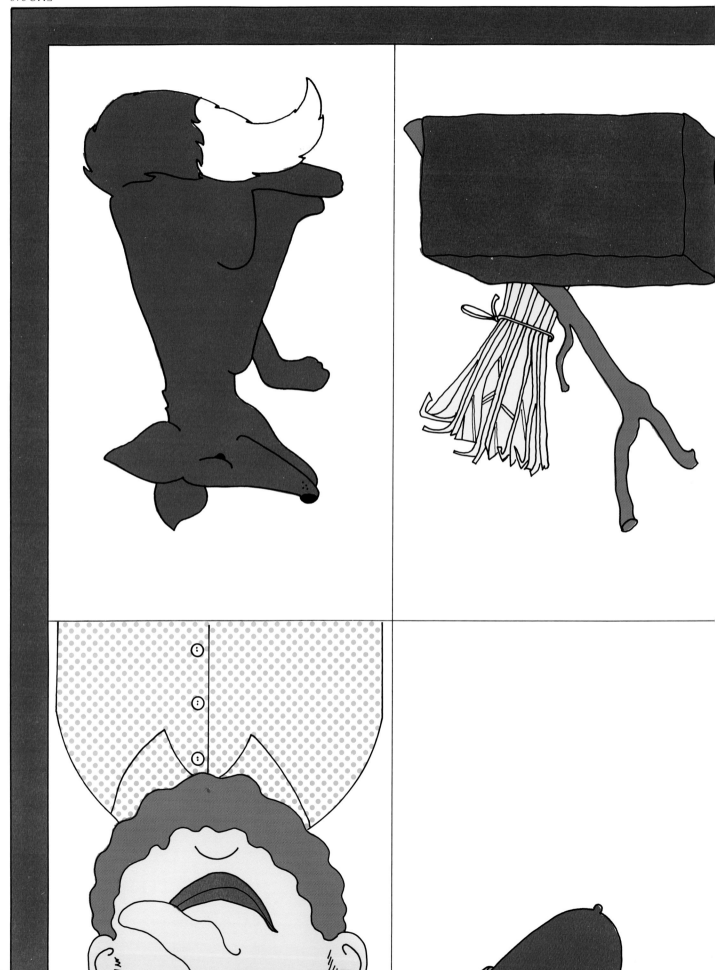

together?

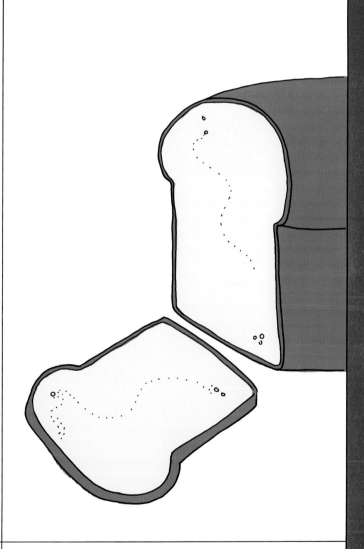

Teacher: Children color and cut out Foxy Loxy's cave and the characters in the story. Slip the strip of characters through the cave opening. Notice that Henny Penny's picture cannot pass through the opening. She was the lucky one.

Henny Penny

out

in

Foxy Loxy

Henny Penny went home.

Teacher: Children cut apart the pictures and paste them in the correct order on a second piece of paper. This is a good time to bake bread in class and to have a "tasting" time of the different types of bread eaten in other countries.

The Little Red Hen

Teacher: Children look for the fairy tale characters hidden in the picture. They may **X** or color the characters they find.

11

_____'s Book
of
Fairy Tales

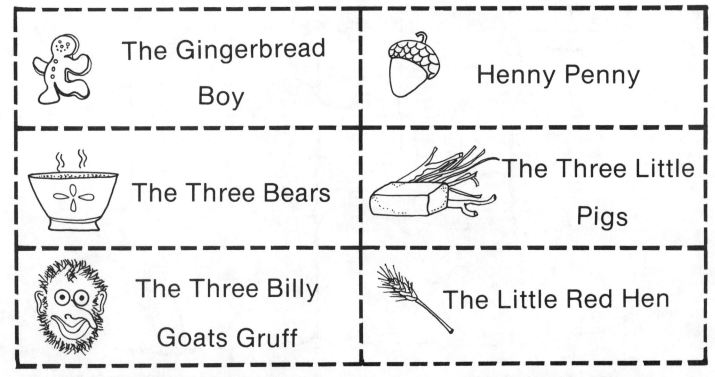

The Gingerbread Boy

Henny Penny

The Three Bears

The Three Little Pigs

The Three Billy Goats Gruff

The Little Red Hen

Teacher: The directions for this page are on page 1.

FUN WITH FAIRY TALES

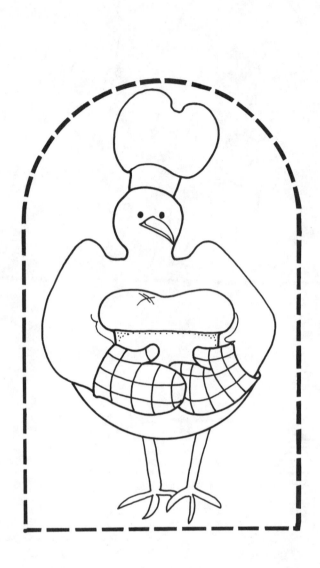